PLAYGROUND BULLY

By Marcia Thornton Jones and Debbie Dadey

Illustrated by Amy Wummer

SCHOLASTIC INC.

New York Toronto London Auckland Sydney
Mexico City New Delhi Hong Kong Buenos Aires

To the friendliest dog I've ever had, my good
buddy Bailey
—DD

To all my four-footed furry best friends and to
people dedicated to keeping them healthy and
happy, especially the compassionate people at
the Lexington Hospital for Cats
—MTJ

ISBN 0-439-30568-3

12 11 10 9 8 7 6 5   2 3 4 5 6/0

Printed in the U.S.A.   40

First Scholastic printing, September 2001

This book is set in 14-point Cheltenham.

Contents

JACK, THE WONDER DOG

JINGLE. JINGLE. I knew that sound. My leash! I dashed through the apartment and crashed right into my human.

"Calm down, Jack," Maggie said with a giggle. I knew Maggie was ready to go to that place she calls school. She wore her baseball cap and backpack. My tail wagged so hard it bumped a table. It wasn't my fault the table was a little wobbly and the flowers fell over. My tail always gets extra excited when Maggie talks to me, especially when she's holding my leash. My leash meant one thing. We were going for a walk.

"Oh, Jack," she said. "What a mess." This time, Maggie didn't sound so happy. "My plan better work."

Plan? What was Maggie talking about?

I stood still long enough for Maggie to snap the leash onto my collar, then I sprinted out the door. Maggie had no choice but to run behind me.

When we got outside, I stuck my nose in the air and breathed in the heavenly smell of a rotten burger lying in the gutter. I stopped sniffing. Something was wrong. Maggie was heading the wrong way.

It was up to me to keep Maggie from getting lost. I might be a shaggy dog. I might have fleas. But you *can't* say I forget to watch out for Maggie! I don't want to brag, but I consider myself Jack, the Wonder Dog.

I did what any good Wonder Dog would do. I sat down, refusing to budge.

"Come on, Jack," Maggie said in that too kind voice that usually meant a trip to the vet. I wasn't going to fall for it this time. Not me. I'm too smart for that. I plopped down on the sidewalk and put my head on my front paws.

"But this will be fun," Maggie said, giving my leash a firm tug. "Like going to the park."

Park? I lifted my head. I knew all about the park. The park meant running with Maggie and fetching balls. It meant barking at bicycles and chasing squirrels. I liked the park. If wherever we were going was as good as the park, then it was good enough for me. I barked to let her know I understood and leaped to her side.

Unfortunately, when I jumped up, I didn't see the old lady—the one I knocked down. It wasn't just any old lady, either. It was Miss Frimple, the human that lived across the hall from us.

Miss Frimple wasn't exactly beautiful to begin with, but Miss Frimple sprawled on the sidewalk was definitely not a pretty sight. Even I couldn't help noticing her underwear had little blue flowers all over them. Miss Frimple has that ticklish kind of smell that makes a dog want to bark. So I did.

"Get that dog away from me," Miss

Frimple snapped, and she kicked at my leash. Of course, I was at the end of that very same leash, so I did what any self-respecting dog would do. I barked again.

"Hush, Jack," Maggie said as she helped Miss Frimple up.

Miss Frimple smoothed her skirt back down over her flowered underwear and hissed, "That dog is a menace to this neighborhood."

Now, hissing makes any dog's hair stand up on end, including mine. So, naturally, I barked once again.

"I'm sorry," Maggie said. "We didn't see you coming."

"It's bad enough that dog's barking disturbs my soap operas," Miss Frimple said. "But now he has the nerve to trip me on my very own sidewalk. This is the last straw!"

I let out a little whine to tell Miss Frimple that barking is what all good watchdogs do. Whenever Maggie and her grown-up people were gone, I made sure everybody knew Jack, the Wonder Dog was on duty.

"You don't have to worry about his barking anymore," Maggie said in her polite voice. She always talked that way when she was around grown-ups. "I have a plan."

"Well, it's about time," Miss Frimple snarled and stomped away. "I hope your plan includes getting rid of that beast," she called over her shoulder.

Getting rid of me? How could she? Maggie and I had been together since I was nothing more than a pup. We belonged together.

I was so busy worrying that I didn't notice where Maggie was taking me. Sure, I rushed ahead like always, pulling Maggie from one pole to another. Of course, pulling Maggie isn't hard, since she's a little on the short side. But my heart really wasn't into sniffing. I was too worried.

We didn't go far. Not like we do on a real walk. Instead, Maggie stopped in front of a low building that was just around the corner and down the block from our apartment. "We're here," she said.

I wasn't sure where we were, but it had a strange smell. One thing for sure, it definitely wasn't the park.

THE BULLY

"This is your new school," Maggie said. "You'll be going to school every day to learn everything a dog needs to know. No more broken vases. No more neighbor complaints. It's the perfect plan!"

I swallowed hard. School? I'd heard about school from Maggie and her friends. School meant studying. It meant practicing. School meant homework. Who would protect Maggie and our apartment if I were gone all day? Being a Wonder Dog is busy work. I didn't have time for school. Nope, I decided—no school for me. I planted my feet firmly on the sidewalk.

"You *are* going to dog school, Jack," Maggie said, dragging me up the steps. Let me tell you something, being dragged by a human is humiliating for a Wonder Dog like me. She finally stopped in front of two big brown muddy shoes. I couldn't help myself. I had to sniff.

"This is Fred Barkley. He'll take good care of you," Maggie told me.

Fred rubbed my left ear. "Welcome," he said.

Maggie turned to leave and so did I, but Fred had a firm hold on my leash. "Wait!" I barked to Maggie.

Fred tugged on the leash. "Hush," Fred said. "No barking allowed in the building."

No barking? What kind of place was this? Didn't he know that barking was the best way to tell the world everything it needed to know? I barked once more, trying to make Fred understand.

Fred shook his head. "Maggie was right," he said. "You're going to be a tough pup to crack."

I barked at the word pup. Being full-grown made me a dog—a Wonder Dog, to be exact. I barked once to tell Fred how old I was.

Fred didn't get it. He smiled a big smile

that showed his dull teeth. "I can be just as stubborn as you," he warned. "Now, heel."

Why did this human want me to look at the back of his foot all of a sudden? I glanced down. Nothing special there, though his shoes did look rather tasty. The thought of chewing on one made me lick my lips. There's nothing better than an old leather shoe.

"It looks like we have a lot of work to do," Fred said with a sigh. "We'll start right after recess. Let's go."

Fred didn't know he was dealing with Jack, the Wonder Dog. I didn't plan on going anywhere. I sat down.

I may be stubborn, but I'm not as strong as Fred. He pulled me down a long hallway, talking about his feet the entire way. "Heel. Heel," he kept saying. The floor was slick, and my paws slipped along behind him.

Doors lined the hallway, and from behind each door came a flood of smells. One room smelled like kibble. I dug my nails in, trying to get him to stop there. No such luck. Fred didn't stop until we were at the end of the hallway. He opened a door. I sniffed. I knew those smells. TREES! GRASS! DOGS!

Quicker than a dog can scratch a flea, Fred pushed me outside and unclipped the leash. "You're lucky," he said. "You came at recess."

I didn't feel lucky. I tried following Fred back down the hallway. I didn't get the chance. Fred slammed the door, leaving me in a big yard surrounded by a tall brick wall. Bushes grew in the corners, and dirty rags were piled in the shade. All of a sudden the pile of rags started moving. I jumped back, ready to attack any monster. Instead of a monster, an old basset hound blinked one sleepy eye at me. "How do you do?" he asked, his words slow and low like the buzz of a bee. "My name is Woodrow."

"I'm Jack," I said. "Where am I?"

Woodrow glanced around the yard, his long ears sweeping the ground. "This is Barkley's School for Dogs, the best school in town. Dogs from Barkley's have even been known to become champs at running tunnels, jumping bars, and balancing on the teeter-totter. I won a few trophies back in my prime."

I looked around the yard. Bright benches and tunnels were scattered around. A lopsided teeter-totter was perched near the side of the yard. This place would be fun if Maggie was with me. Anything was fun with Maggie.

Maggie. I had to get back to the apartment before she got home from school. She needed me to protect her.

"I don't need to be a champion at a dog show," I told Woodrow. "I already have a job. I protect the best human in the world. I belong with my one and only friend."

Woodrow yawned. "You can make friends wherever you go. Besides, at Barkley's School for Dogs you'll learn to be the best," he said. "My advice is to grab a nap whenever you can." With those words, Woodrow dropped his snout to his paws and closed his eyes.

I needed something to chew on. Chewing helps a dog think. A big bone or a nice smelly shoe to sink my teeth into would do the trick.

The only thing I found worth chewing was a dirty squeak toy. It would have to do. The toy was full of great smells and it felt good to my sharp teeth. I must have really been concentrating on it because I didn't smell them coming. Suddenly, two huge paws the color of dirt planted themselves right in front of my nose.

Now, I'm not what you'd call a big dog. I'm not exactly little, either, but these paws made mine look tiny. I stared up into the face of a large Doberman with a notch missing from one ear. "Hi!" I whined, just to be friendly. I'm not sure she understood, considering the toy was in my mouth.

This dog wasn't interested in being pals. "Give me my toy," she growled.

A little bulldog grinned from the shadows of the big dog. He had stubby

legs, and his head was so big it looked like he had trouble holding it up. "Yeah, yeah," the bulldog panted. "Give back the toy."

"I'll take care of this, Clyde," the big dog snapped. Then looking at me, she growled again. "I said, give me my toy."

"Sorry, I don't see your name on it," I growled. I realized how smart-alecky that sounded. I knew for a Fido Fact that growling was not the best way to make friends, but something about this big dog made the hair on my back stiffen. The big dog grabbed for the toy. Instinct made me hang on tight.

Tug-of-war! Maggie and I played it all the time, but not like this. The Doberman wasn't interested in fun. She wanted that toy and it didn't matter if she had to pull out my teeth to get it. She twirled me around the yard like a yo-yo on a string.

"Fight! Fight!" Clyde yelped, hopping up and down on his tiny legs.

This big dog and her slobbering side-kick were enough to make any dog growl. So I did. Of course, that made me lose my death grip on the toy.

I flew off and landed with a clang against the teeter-totter. The big dog trotted off like a victor on the battlefield, her head held high and the toy hanging from her slobbering jowls. Clyde waddled as fast as he could behind her.

I did what any self-respecting mutt would do in the situation. I barked just to let that bully of a dog and her sidekick know I hadn't given up. What a big mistake!

BiG MiSTAKE

The man with the muddy shoes shot out the back door. I could tell that meant trouble. A dog knows these things just by watching feet hit the ground. Fred's feet landed so heavily near my paws that I naturally hunkered down and whined.

"Maggie was right," Fred said. "You have one loud bark."

My tail double-thumped with hope. Finally, I'd found someone who appreciated my Wonder Dog bark. I lifted my head and treated Fred to a howl loud enough to stop a bus.

Fred slapped a hand around my snout, cutting my beautiful song short. He leaned down until his nose almost touched mine. I tried to back away, but his grip on my nose tightened. Then he said THE WORD. The word that stops dogs dead in their tracks.

"NO!"

Just to make me feel even worse, he repeated it.

"NO!"

Finally, Fred let go of my nose. "Now, be quiet. Recess is almost over. Then you and I are going to practice walking on a leash," he said before disappearing back into the big building.

I glanced at Woodrow. He blinked his big brown eyes. "Don't worry. First impressions aren't everything," Woodrow told me. "Things will get better."

I whined. This day was turning into a doggy nightmare. Maggie left me in this strange place. A monster dog took my toy. And now, Fred hated me. School definitely wasn't for me. I wanted to go home.

I decided to do the next best thing. Hide.

"Pssst."

I turned in a complete circle. I didn't see anyone. Then I heard it again.

"Pssst. Ober hereb."

I perked up my Wonder Dog ears and zeroed in on the sound. There, behind three garbage cans, was a black nose. I trotted over to investigate. A spotted beagle with droopy ears and a soggy tennis ball wedged in the side of his mouth huddled behind the cans. Next to the beagle sat the most beautiful white poodle I'd ever set my brown eyes on.

The droopy-eared beagle dropped his tennis ball. It landed near his paws with a splat. He sniffed me good and nodded. "No missing clumps of hair. Ears still in one piece. Howl-a-rrific!" he said. "I'd call you one lucky dog."

"My name is Jack," I barked.

The poodle nosed her way to the front, her gem-studded collar gleaming in the sunlight. "Excuse his rude sniff," she said, "but he's a beagle, and sniffing is what beagles do best. Welcome to Barkley's

School. My name is Blondie. The dog with the ball is Floyd."

I nodded at Floyd but kept one eye on Blondie.

Floyd's lip curled up over one pointed tooth in a crooked grin. "We thought you were a goner."

"Goner?" I asked. "What are you talking about?"

Blondie peered under my belly to get a good look at the yard before whispering, "We're talking about Sweetcakes."

"Sweetcakes?" I asked, my mouth watering. "That sounds good. I could use a bite of cake. Or cookie. Even pudding would do."

"You may get a bite, all right," Floyd said. "A bite in the behind, if you're not careful."

"Sweetcakes is the name of that brute with the toy," Blondie explained. "She's Fred's championship dog. There's an entire wall in the school plastered with ribbons she's won at dog shows."

Floyd looked at the playground equipment. "Sweetcakes can leap those bars, dart through tunnels, and walk across the teeter-totter faster than any dog alive," he said.

"She rules this school yard," Blondie added. "So you'd better get used to it."

"Sweetcakes is a mean, lean fighting machine. We do whatever she says,"

Floyd told me. "Didn't you notice her ear? It was ripped in a fight."

Blondie nodded. "Bad as she looks, the other dog looked even worse."

I sighed. Suddenly, all the strength seeped out of my legs. I collapsed on the ground and whined. "I'll never get used to this place. I have to get home so I can protect Maggie."

"There's no way out," Floyd said. He was hard to understand because he'd started chewing on his tennis ball again. It sounded like, "Mure's no bay ouyee."

Blondie touched my nose with hers. "Don't worry. The humans always come back," she said softly. "Maggie will be back for you, too."

"I hope you're right," I said.

"If I were you, I'd forget about Maggie," Floyd said, "and worry about what's coming across the school yard instead!"

COWARDS

Sweetcakes marched around the jumping bars and hopped over a tunnel, the chew toy still swinging from her mouth. Clyde waddled along behind Sweetcakes, his stubby legs working double-time just to keep up. They stopped right in front of me, and Sweetcakes dropped the toy on the ground. I thought about grabbing it, but Sweetcakes held it down with a paw. I noticed her black toenails were in need of a serious trim.

"Listen up, one and all," Sweetcakes

howled. Black noses, droopy ears, and shaggy tails appeared all over the school yard. Two Irish setters poked their heads out of one of the tunnels. A dachshund crawled from beneath a bush. A shaggy white Westie popped out of one of the tunnels. A black-and-white terrier with a smushed-in nose crept out of behind a shed in the back of the yard. At least seventeen other dogs crawled out from hiding places. Even Woodrow lifted his head from his paws.

"Nobody plays with the new guy," Sweetcakes growled. "And I mean NOBODY!"

"Yeah," Clyde panted with a grin. "No one."

"You can't tell us what to do," I said. "We're not afraid of you, are we?" I didn't hear a sound. "Guys?" I glanced over my shoulders. "Guys?"

There wasn't a dog in sight. Every last

cowardly dog had found a hiding place. Even Woodrow disappeared into his pile of rags.

Sweetcakes took a step closer to me, the muscles in her back legs ready to spring. Her lips curled up to show both glistening yellow fangs. "What did you say?" Sweetcakes growled.

I looked at her scissor-sharp fangs and figured Jack, the Wonder Dog was about to go down in a blaze of glory. I got ready for the fight to end all fights.

Sweetcakes held her nose high in the air and sniffed. She turned a complete circle and sniffed again.

"I smell something rotten," she said, "something besides Jack."

Clyde sniffed. "Yeah, yeah. Something rotten."

I couldn't help myself. I sniffed, too. Sweetcakes was right. Something new was in the air, and for some reason it made me feel even more homesick.

"I know that smell," Sweetcakes growled. "It's CAT!"

"Cat! Yeah, yeah! Cat," Clyde panted.

Sweetcakes, with her nose to the ground, forgot all about me. She sniffed out a zigzag trail across the yard. She stopped next to the teeter-totter and howled a battle cry.

Clyde ran around Sweetcakes and

barked. "Calling all dogs! Calling all dogs!"

Twenty dogs leaped from their hiding places and ran to Sweetcakes's side. They came from beneath bushes, inside tunnels, and even behind the garbage cans. Only Woodrow didn't go to Sweetcakes. Woodrow lifted one droopy ear for a split second. Then he went back to his nap.

"What do you want us to do, Sweetcakes?" one of the Irish setters asked.

"We'll do anything," the dachshund added. "Just name it."

"Anything," the white mop of a Westie yipped.

"You will find that cat," Sweetcakes told the dogs, with slobber dripping from her jowls, "if it's the last thing you do. And if you don't find the cat," she added, "it *will* be the last thing you do!"

CAT

I didn't know which was worse—Sweetcakes or cats. I'd never really dealt with a cat before, but it was a Fido Fact that dogs are supposed to hate cats. If you had asked me yesterday, I wouldn't have thought twice. I would've put my nose to the ground and found that cat faster than you could scratch a flea.

Sweetcakes changed everything. Hunting with her was like going to the vet to get a shot with a twelve-inch-long needle. Even Blondie sniffed the ground in search of the cat. Floyd still had his soggy ball in his mouth, but he had his nose close to the ground. He sniffed so hard he sneezed. His tennis ball flew from his mouth and bounced across the yard. He darted after it, grabbed it in his mouth, then took off sniffing again.

The other dogs hunted, too. They spread out around the trees, tunnels, and benches. The Westie scurried under bellies and between legs. A small brown dog with a bald spot on his rump and a Chihuahua dodged the bigger dogs.

Woodrow and I were the only dogs standing still. Actually, Woodrow wasn't even standing. "Why aren't you falling for this, Woodrow?" I asked.

Woodrow lifted his heavy head. He glanced with sad brown eyes at the pack of dogs making their way across Barkley's yard. "Sweetcakes isn't worth my time," he finally said.

"I thought Sweetcakes made all the decisions around here," I said. "Why doesn't she bother you?"

"Sweetcakes is a bully," Woodrow said. "Bullies can only be a bully if they have someone to push around. I don't let Sweetcakes bully me. She knows it. Besides, I have no reason to hate a cat just for being a cat."

Woodrow yawned as if our conversa-

tion had drained his last ounce of energy. "Nap time is almost over," he reminded me. "You're going to need all your energy for Fred's assignments. Better get some shut-eye before it's too late." He then lowered his head back to his paws. A split second later he snored.

I stared at Woodrow. This was no ordinary lazy dog. He was one smart hound. No one bothered him, not even Sweetcakes. Somehow, Woodrow gave me the strength I needed to make up my own mind. If Woodrow wasn't afraid of Sweetcakes, then neither was I.

No dog was the boss of Jack, the Wonder Dog. Especially Sweetcakes. I wasn't about to let her force me into joining her little game of terror. I planted my rump on the ground, determined not to move a muscle.

Besides, there was something about that cat smell. Something very familiar. If only I could figure out where I had smelled that cat before.

I needed a good chewing bone to help me think. I looked down on the ground. There was Sweetcakes's toy. My mouth watered and my tongue reached down. I could almost taste the squeak toy, but then I spied something even better.

By the back door of the school lay two delicious-looking muddy shoes. A tasty leather shoe just might do the trick. I trotted to the door and sank my teeth into the closest shoe. The taste of leather started my mouth watering. Drool covered the toe, making the leather moist and chewable.

As I was biting through the toe of the shoe, the back door opened, and a long shadow threw me into darkness.

DEAD DOG

Fred towered over me like a monster. "What's going on out here?" he yelled.

The rest of the dogs stopped in mid-sniff and looked back at Fred. Even Sweetcakes. One look at Fred, and Sweetcakes turned into a different dog. She bounded across the yard and hopped up, placing her giant paws on Fred's shoulders.

"Now, Sweetcakes," Fred said softly. "You know better than to jump on people." Fred gently pushed Sweetcakes down to the ground and scratched her one good ear. "Good dog, Sweetcakes."

Fred looked down at me. I held the shoe proudly in my mouth and wagged my tail to say hello. Fred did not look happy.

He shook his finger at my nose and said that terrible word again. "NO!" Then, he did something that made me drop that delicious shoe so fast it bounced. Fred

thumped me right on top of my nose with his finger.

Ouch! My nose stung. Even worse, it hurt my heart. I lay down and sighed as Fred snapped a leash to my collar. "Chewing shoes earns you a time-out," he said in a deep voice. He said "time-out" extra loud, and I heard Sweetcakes snickering.

Fred tugged on the leash and marched me right past Blondie, Floyd, Woodrow, and the rest of the dogs.

"Dead dog walking," Sweetcakes said with a mean laugh just loud enough for dogs to hear.

"Dead. Yeah, yeah," Clyde panted from beside Sweetcakes.

"Dead?" I whimpered. "It was only a shoe. And it wasn't a very good one."

"But it was Fred's shoe," Sweetcakes said, trotting behind me. "And now Fred is going to put you out of all your misery!"

"Don't listen to her," Blondie yelped. Sweetcakes snarled at Blondie. Blondie's voice shook a little, but she ignored Sweetcakes. "It's only time-out. You'll be back."

Fred pulled me behind a little shed at the back of the yard. He tied my leash around a tree. "Sit here and think about what you did," Fred said, shaking his finger in front of my nose again. I backed away until my tail smashed against the wall.

Fred disappeared around the shed, leaving me all alone. I waited for him to come back. When he didn't, I tried to run after him. Unfortunately, I forgot about the leash and ended up sitting down hard on the ground.

"That wasn't the smartest thing I've ever seen," a high-pitched voice said. "Of course, you *are* a dog, and dogs aren't the smartest creatures on this green earth."

"Who said that?" I asked. I looked for the voice's owner, turning in a circle. When I did, the leash wrapped around my legs. I fell face first and scraped my chin on the ground.

"Now that was better than watching a three-hour movie," the voice said. "Can you do any other doggy tricks?"

Someone was watching my every move. Who was this spy at Barkley's School?

TAZZ

I rolled on my back, trying to free my legs. That's when I saw her. It was no spy. This was worse. Much worse. It was a cat. The black-and-gold cat stood bigger than most terriers and was as shaggy as a mop. She perched on top of the brick wall, lazily swishing her bushy tail back and forth.

"You're in the wrong place at the wrong time," I growled.

"Believe me, Buster. This wasn't my choice," she said.

"My name isn't Buster," I told her. "It's Jack."

"Whatever," the cat said. She licked a paw and wiped it over one of her ears. "My name is Razzmatazz, but my friends call me Tazz."

If Sweetcakes saw this cat, she would be history. Not that I cared about the cat, but I didn't want to give Sweetcakes anything. "You better hightail it back home. You have no friends here," I warned her.

Tazz sighed. "You are so right," she said. "I was catnapped this very morning. It was horrible! I was able to escape. But now I'm lost."

Those words proved that dogs are smarter than cats. A dog would be able to sniff his way home in no time. "Who would want to catnap you?" I asked.

"A cat burglar, of course," Tazz told me in a bored voice. "Usually there's a dog that lives in my building that scares away burglars," she explained. "He always barks. And I mean always. But for some reason, the dog didn't hear the burglar today."

I couldn't help but smile. I never would let a burglar near Maggie's apartment. "Why would a burglar steal a cat?" I asked.

Tazz walked along the top of the brick wall, swishing her tail back and forth. The sun glinted off her sparkling collar and the gold in her fur glistened in the sun. "Who wouldn't be impressed by such beauty?" she purred.

Of course, I was not the least bit impressed, but I felt sorry for Tazz when she started crying. "More than anything," she whimpered, "I want to go home. I miss having my ears scratched and being able to sharpen my claws on the sofa."

I knew about being homesick. I wanted to go home, too. Thinking about how Maggie scratched my own ears made me sigh.

"What's worse," Tazz said, "is that the cat burglar is hot on my tail!"

My supersensitive Wonder Dog ears picked up the sound of footsteps on the other side of the wall. "Here, kitty, kitty, kitty," a raspy voice cooed. Two hands gripped the top of the wall. One of the hands reached for Tazz. It could only be one person. The cat burglar! I knew what I had to do, even if it meant helping a cat.

"Jump!" I told Tazz. The cat jumped into the yard next to me. "It's Jack, the Wonder Dog to the rescue. You're safe here," I told her, but I was wrong. I had forgotten about one problem—one huge, ugly, and downright mean problem.

Sweetcakes roared around the corner with the whole pack of dogs behind her. Tazz squeezed up behind me. Sweetcakes took one look and accused me of being the worst thing one dog can say to another.

"A cat lover! Jack's a CAT LOVER!"

"Look, look," Clyde panted from beside Sweetcakes. "The new guy's a cat lover!"

All the other dogs gasped. Floyd dropped his ball. Blondie stared at me. I didn't like the look in her eyes. After all, I'm a normal dog. I know I'm not supposed to care for cats, but Tazz wasn't just any cat. Tazz was lost and in danger. She needed help. Jack, the Wonder Dog didn't need to know any more.

Sweetcakes moved closer and growled, showing every pointed tooth in her mouth. "You've chewed your last toy and sniffed your last fire hydrant," Sweetcakes said.

Like Woodrow said, there was no reason to hate a cat just for being a cat. But I had plenty of reasons not to like Sweetcakes. I stood my ground and prepared to defend Tazz, even if it was the last thing I ever did.

THE LAST
DoGGy NERVE

Sweetcakes moved closer to Tazz and me. I felt the hair on my back bristle. I heard Tazz hiss. I waited for Sweetcakes to lunge. A voice stopped her cold.

"Now how did a cat get in here?" Fred asked.

Dogs scattered in all directions, making a path for Fred as he walked around the shed. Fred unhooked me and snatched Tazz up from the ground.

Sweetcakes whined and hurried to lick Fred's elbow. "Good girl," Fred said, patting

Sweetcakes on the head. "You found this poor lost little kitty."

Fred was wrong about at least two things. Tazz was definitely not little, and Sweetcakes had nothing to do with finding the cat. It made me lose my Wonder Dog appetite to see Sweetcakes acting nice and taking credit for finding Tazz. Just a second ago Sweetcakes had been ready to eat Tazz alive.

"I'd better find this cat's owner," Fred said, looking at Tazz's collar for a tag. "Then it's back to work for the rest of you!" Without so much as a pat on my Wonder Dog head, Fred hurried across the yard with Sweetcakes at his heels.

Most of the other dogs went back to their shady spots. I peeked around the corner of the shed. Blondie and Floyd joined me in time to see Fred stop at the back door of Barkley's School. He turned and held a hand out to

Sweetcakes. "Stay," he said firmly. "Stay."

Sweetcakes sat down and stared up at Fred. "Good, doggy," Fred said. Then he took Tazz inside, leaving Sweetcakes sitting at the door.

"How can he believe Sweetcakes is a good dog?" I said, glaring at Blondie and Floyd. "And how can you be Sweetcakes's friend?"

Blondie looked at the ground. "You know we're not her friend."

"We're your friend," Floyd said.

"You could have fooled me," I snapped.

Floyd scratched one of his big brown ears. "It's just that Sweetcakes told us not to play with you."

"We don't like it, but we always do what she says," Blondie admitted.

"Even if it's wrong?" I asked.

Blondie started to answer, but Fred came out the door with a bag in one hand and a bell in the other. Fred rang the bell and shouted, "Training time!" All the dogs barked and raced to Fred, even Blondie and Floyd. I trotted over out of curiosity.

I sniffed as I got closer. My Wonder Dog nose zeroed in on the bag in Fred's hand. "Are those treats?" I asked, my mouth already starting to water. I reached up and tried to snatch the bag.

Fred was quick. He jerked the bag out of my reach. "You have to earn these treats," he told me with a laugh.

Do people have to earn their cookies? Earn candy bars? Do they earn their French fries? No. So why did he think a dog had to earn yum-yums?

First, Fred made us stand in a line. Well, most of us stood. Some of the younger dogs rolled around, and Woodrow slept. One by one, Fred told us each to sit. Most of us had learned that at home. When it was my turn, I sat like a champ. Fred patted me on the head, and I grinned.

"Let's try some other tricks," Fred said, reaching into his bag and pulling out a handful of tidbits.

"Treats! Treats!" Floyd woofed. All the dogs leaned closer to Fred, but not a single dog tried to take a snack from Fred's hand. Instead, they looked at Sweetcakes.

Blondie nudged me back with her slender nose. "Wait a minute. Sweetcakes always gets to go first."

I watched as Sweetcakes stood up on

her long hind legs and earned a treat.

The white Westie rolled over and earned the next treat.

"Fred thinks he's training us, but we're really training him," Blondie told me. "Watch this." She walked on her hind legs toward Fred and earned a treat.

"See," Blondie said, "it's easy."

Easy if you can walk on your hind legs, I thought. I couldn't. The treats looked good. My mouth watered and I whined. How was I going to get a treat?

"You couldn't do a trick if your life depended on it," Sweetcakes said with a sneer.

That's when I showed Sweetcakes that I knew how to shake hands like a politician on a presidential campaign trail. I sat in front of Fred and lifted my right paw. Fred shook it and gave me not one, but two treats.

Fred grabbed Floyd's ball out of his mouth and tossed it. "Fetch," Fred told Floyd. Floyd ran, but came back with a stick. Fred gave him a treat anyway.

Working for yum-yums is harder than it looks. Fred had us sitting, shaking hands, fetching, and then he even tried making us walk on leashes. As soon as he clipped the leash on me I figured it meant a romp in the park, so I pulled Fred as hard as I could. I didn't get far.

"Heel," Fred said sternly. I looked back at his shoes. This was the second time in one day this human mentioned the back of his foot. I stopped tugging on my leash long enough to lick his shoe for him. I didn't get any yum-yums for that.

"That's enough for now!" Fred finally said with a sigh. "It's lunchtime."

In a few minutes, Fred was back with a big bag of kibble. He rang his bell and shouted, "Come and eat!" I started toward Fred, but Blondie held me back with a silky white paw.

"Not yet," she said.

Sweetcakes sauntered up to one of the huge metal food bowls. As soon as Fred filled it, Sweetcakes slowly ate her lunch. My stomach growled. The yum-yum treats had made me even hungrier. "Come on," I said. "Let's eat."

"Don't you get it?" Floyd told me, his big ears swinging. "We have to wait for Sweetcakes to finish." Every other dog waited for Sweetcakes to finish her lunch. Even Woodrow, who lumbered over next to me, didn't make a move for a food bowl.

This Sweetcakes stuff was getting on my last doggy nerve. "That's not right," I told Floyd, but Blondie calmed me down.

"Don't worry. You'll get used to it just like we all did. It's not so bad," Blondie told me. "Everything will be all right."

"Everything may be all right for us," Woodrow interrupted with a nod toward the back door, "but it's not okay for the cat."

Fred had forgotten to shut the door tight behind him. When Sweetcakes finished eating, she used her nose to push the door all the way open. Sweetcakes bared her teeth and growled. "No cat is allowed in Barkley's. Ever!"

Before anybody could stop her, Sweetcakes hightailed it toward Tazz.

9

HAIRBALL

"This has gone far enough," I told the gang. "Follow me!"

Blondie, Floyd, and I raced into the building after Sweetcakes. Even Woodrow nosed his way in the door and followed. Clyde chased after all of us.

"What're you going to do?" Floyd asked me with the tennis ball in his mouth. It sounded like, "Vot r yog doga-du?"

I shrugged. I had no idea what to do. But I knew that I had to find Sweetcakes. Our claws clattered down the long hallway to the big front room. That's where we found Sweetcakes. And Tazz.

Tazz hissed from a chair at Sweetcakes.

"How come the cat gets to be on a chair?" Floyd complained, dropping his ball. "That's not fair."

Sweetcakes smiled at us. "I'm glad you're here. We'll make that cat sorry she ever set a single paw in Barkley's School for Dogs."

"Sorry. Yeah, yeah," Clyde panted.

Sweetcakes growled and moved closer to Tazz.

Tazz may be a cat, but she hadn't hurt a single flea on my head. I knew if somebody didn't do something fast Tazz would end up as a hairball in Sweetcakes's mouth. Jack, the Wonder Dog couldn't let that happen.

Tazz arched her back as Sweetcakes lunged. That's when I closed my eyes and jumped. Sweetcakes and I crashed in midair. We tumbled to the ground just as the front door opened.

"It's the cat burglar!" Tazz yowled.

I opened my eyes and saw a big man. Beside him stood the one and only Miss Frimple. "It's that beast!" she shouted, pointing a bony finger at me. "Grab him!"

That's when I saw Maggie coming up the steps behind Miss Frimple. More than anything, I wanted to run straight into Maggie's arms, but a Wonder Dog must do his job. Besides, the cat burglar caught me off guard when he yelled, "Get that cat!"

The cat burglar lunged for Tazz, but so did Sweetcakes. "Run! Run! Run!" I barked to Tazz.

"Will someone quiet that barking dog!" Miss Frimple screamed at me. Tazz sprang into action. She jumped past me, darted under Sweetcakes, and knocked Clyde into a corner.

Tazz zipped down the hallway with Sweetcakes close behind. At the sound of the commotion, Fred came into the hallway. Tazz dodged Fred, but Sweetcakes wasn't fast enough. She slammed right into him. Fred landed on the floor. Sweetcakes was too intent on catching the cat to realize what she'd done. She scrambled up and raced after Tazz. The rest of us dogs jumped over Fred. The cat burglar, Miss Frimple, and Maggie helped Fred stand up.

Tazz galloped down the hall and skidded into the kibble room. Sweetcakes followed her. Cornered, the cat backed away from the Doberman and ended up next to a huge bag of treats. Sweetcakes crouched in front of her, ready to spring. I came into the room so fast I couldn't stop. I slid out of control, right past Sweetcakes and into Tazz.

"Yow!" Tazz screeched as she tumbled into the treat bag. "What are you doing?"

"It's Jack, the Wonder Dog to the rescue," I explained. "I'm saving you."

Tazz licked her shoulder. "Well, you're not doing very well. I think you scuffed my fur."

"Move out of the way," Sweetcakes growled at me. Slobber made her fangs glisten. "I'm taking care of that feline clump of fur once and for all."

This looked like the end of me—and Tazz. What I didn't count on were my friends.

Blondie, Floyd, and Woodrow trotted into the kibble room. This time, Floyd wasn't carrying his soggy ball. Instead, Sweetcakes's toy dangled from his teeth. As usual, Woodrow didn't seem too interested in any of us. Instead, he wandered over to a bag of kibble.

"This is no time to think about food," I said under my breath.

Woodrow slowly shook his head. "This, my friend, is the perfect time," he told me.

"Hey, big girl," Blondie snapped. "That sure looks like a yummy-tasting toy Floyd found."

Sweetcakes took one look at Floyd with her toy and lunged. At that moment, Woodrow calmly nudged the food bag. The huge bag tumbled to the floor, sending dog food everywhere. Sweetcakes landed right in the middle of the rolling kibble. She tried to get her footing. It was no use. Sweetcakes fell flat on her stubby tail just as Miss Frimple, Maggie, and the cat burglar came in the door. They all slipped on the crunchy treats and crashed to the floor.

"Fang-tastic!" Floyd yelped, dropping the toy. "That's what I call teamwork!"

I took the chance to grab Tazz by the scruff of her neck and run.

OOPS!

"Get my cat from that dog!" Mrs. Frimple yelled as I raced past.

"I'm sorry, Aunt Stella," the cat burglar said. "I'll get Tazz to the vet just like I promised."

My toenails skidded to a stop and I opened my Wonder Dog jaws wide, letting Tazz plop to the floor. I looked at the cat burglar. I looked at Miss Frimple. Then I glared down at Tazz. "Wait a minute. Did that man just call her Aunt Stella? And did Miss Frimple just call you *her* cat?"

Tazz tossed her head. "No one owns me," she meowed. She sounded a bit too smug, if you ask me.

"I thought you said you were being cat-napped," I growled, wondering why Jack, the Wonder Dog had believed anything this cat said.

"Oops," Tazz said. "Sorry about that. It *felt* like I was being catnapped."

I shook my head in disbelief as Miss Frimple's nephew plucked Tazz from the ground. "See you around," Tazz said, twitching her whiskers.

By the grin on Tazz's face, I knew I was not seeing the last of her.

Sweetcakes made one last leap at Tazz, but Fred grabbed the dog's collar. "I'm ashamed of my little baby," Fred said as he snapped a leash on Sweetcakes's collar. "What has gotten into you? This means time-out for you. Your first one ever!"

It sounded like justice had been done. Maybe Jack, the Wonder Dog had succeeded after all. Maggie gave me a big hug. Everything was going to be okay. Maggie had come back for me. I did what all happy dogs do. I barked.

"Hush, Jack," Maggie said, hugging me.

Miss Frimple frowned at me. "That noisy dog has caused me to fall twice in one day."

"I'm sorry," Maggie said. "But Jack did save your cat from that big dog."

"Humph," Miss Frimple said. "He still has that annoying barking problem."

"We'll work on that tomorrow," Fred told us as he pulled Sweetcakes toward the back door.

I gulped. Tomorrow? I had to come back tomorrow?

"Don't worry," Blondie told me. "We'll be here, too."

Floyd nodded, his floppy ears swinging. "I'll even let you play with my tennis ball."

"I thought Sweetcakes said you couldn't play with me," I whimpered to Floyd and Blondie.

"Forget that nonsense," Woodrow said with a yawn, "and remember who your friends are."

"Woodrow is right," Blondie said. "We're friends."

"And friends stick together," Floyd added, smiling his crooked grin.

Woodrow had been right. You can make friends anywhere. "Barkley's School won't be so bad as long as you're here," I told my three new friends.

"Don't be so sure," Sweetcakes barked as Fred dragged her away. "I'll be here, too. And I'll be waiting for you!"

It hadn't been easy, but with a little help from my new friends I had survived my first day at Barkley's School for Dogs. Of course I had. After all, I *am* Jack, the Wonder Dog!